The Shaking Bag

WRITTEN BY Gwendolyn Battle-Lavert
ILLUSTRATED BY Aminah Brenda Lynn Robinson

Albert Whitman & Company
Morton Grove, Illinois

Library of Congress Cataloging-in-Publication Data
Battle-Lavert, Gwendolyn.

The shaking bag / by Gwendolyn Battle-Lavert; Illustrated by Aminah Brenda Lynn
Robinson.
p. cm.
Summary: An old African-American woman willingly shares all she
has and is repaid with a bag that provides for all her needs.
ISBN 0-8075-7328-0
[1. Generosity Fiction. 2. Ravens Fiction.] I. Robinson, Aminah Brenda Lynn, ill. II. Title.
PZ7.B32446Sh   2000
[E] – dc21   99-16974
CIP

Published in 2000 by Albert Whitman & Company,
6340 Oakton Street, Morton Grove, Illinois 60053-2723.
Published simultaneously in Canada
by General Publishing, Limited, Toronto.
Printed in the United States of America.
10 9 8 7 6 5 4 3 2 1

The design is by Scott Piehl.

To Leslie and Lance Lavert.
— G. B-L.

For the little babies born in
1998 and 1999: Kennedy, Kiah,
Dominique, Isaiah, and Quinten.
— A. B. L. R.

Miss Annie Mae lived in an old, run-down house with her trusted dog, Effie Lucille. Miss Annie loved birds, and the yard was filled with birdhouses she'd made for her friends. All kinds of birds lived happily in Miss Annie Mae's yard. She never let them go hungry.

One cold, blustery evening, five ravens landed on her clothesline. They were black as night. Like trapeze artists, they swayed back and forth on the line.

Miss Annie Mae said, "Ya'll just come on down. You've nearly missed your dinner! I've got a few more seeds in this bag—I musta been saving them just for you."

Shake, shake, shake! Seeds fell to the ground.

The five ravens swooped down to get their share.

The north wind dropped to a gentle breeze. When the ravens finished eating, one flew back up on the clothesline. It stared at Miss Annie.

She waved. "Goodnight, friends," she said. "I'll see ya'll tomorrow." She left the empty seed bag and went inside.

She settled down in the only chair she had. For a little while, she read from her old, torn Bible. Then she looked at the small chunk of bread on the table.

Miss Annie Mae frowned. How was she going to feed herself and Effie Lucille? How was she going to get enough food for her birds for the winter? "Well, it's a blessing there's enough for tomorrow," she said to herself.

She cut a slice of bread for herself and one for Effie Lucille. The last slice she put in the cupboard to save for her birds.

Suddenly, Effie's ears popped up. "Wooof! Wooof!" she barked.

Then came a loud knocking. *Tat-tat-tat! Rat-tat-tat!*

Miss Annie Mae picked up the lantern. "I'm a-comin'! Hold your horses!"

She pulled up the latch. The door swung open, and there stood a young man.

"Good evening, Ma'am," he said. "I'm Raven Reed."

His deep, dark eyes seemed to stare into Miss Annie's soul.

"You any kin to the Reeds up the street?" she asked.

"No, Ma'am," said Raven Reed. "All my folks live down south. I'm a trading man. I've seen the world, and now I'm going home. Can you spare me a room for the night?"

"I've never been one to turn a needy soul away. Come on in, child," she said. "By the way, I'm Miss Annie Mae. I'm sorry it's so cold in here."

"Oh, I'll fix that, Ma'am," said Raven Reed. He was holding her old seed bag. He gave that bag a real good shaking. *"Shake it up! Shake it up! All around!"*

All of a sudden, a stack of wood appeared in the old stove. Then a fire sparkled and blazed.

"Oh, mercy me!" said Miss Annie Mae. "I've never seen such as this!"

The room grew toasty warm. "Let's sit down," said Miss Annie. "Please take my chair."

"No, Ma'am," said Raven. "I won't take your only chair."

Again, he took the bag and gave it a shaking. *"Shake it up! Shake it up! All around!"*

Out fell two chairs—a chair for Raven Reed and one for Effie Lucille, too!

Miss Annie Mae said, "This *is* a blessing. Child, you must be hungry. I've got a crust of bread in the cupboard. It's all I have for my birds tomorrow. But we'll make do."

"No, I've got food," said Raven.

He shook the bag. *"Shake it up! Shake it up! All around!"*

Rolling from that sack came fancy hot dogs, mashed potatoes, fried chicken, hard-boiled eggs, sweet peas, a pot of tea, enough catsup and mustard for twenty folks, and a piping-hot apple pie. The small table wobbled from the heavy load.

"Come on, kind lady! Let's eat!" said Raven.

"All this food for such a small table," said Miss Annie Mae. "I'm afraid it's going to fall over."

"Oh, don't worry! I can fix that," said Raven Reed, taking up the bag again. *"Shake it up! Shake it up! All around!"*

The walls shook and cracked.
The room grew wider and taller.
The table grew longer.

"My land," said Miss Annie Mae, sitting down. "I feel like a queen."
Raven gave Effie Lucille a fancy hot dog. Then Miss Annie Mae
and Raven ate and talked and laughed the night away. A feeling
of happiness came over Miss Annie when she looked into Raven's
face. She saw eyes young of age but ancient of spirit.

After supper, Miss Annie Mae made Raven a pallet by the fire. She climbed into bed and slept long and deep. When she woke the next morning, she could smell eggs, ham, toast, and tea. But she didn't think about her own breakfast. Instead, she rushed to the cupboard. "Oh, my goodness, I must feed my birds," she said.

"No need!" said Raven. "All of your friends have been fed. Now it's your turn to eat."

"I've never been treated this royally!" she confessed.

When Miss Annie Mae had finished her breakfast, Raven said, "I must go! There are miles ahead of me."

"I want to give you something," she said. "But I don't have much. Would you take this bag?"

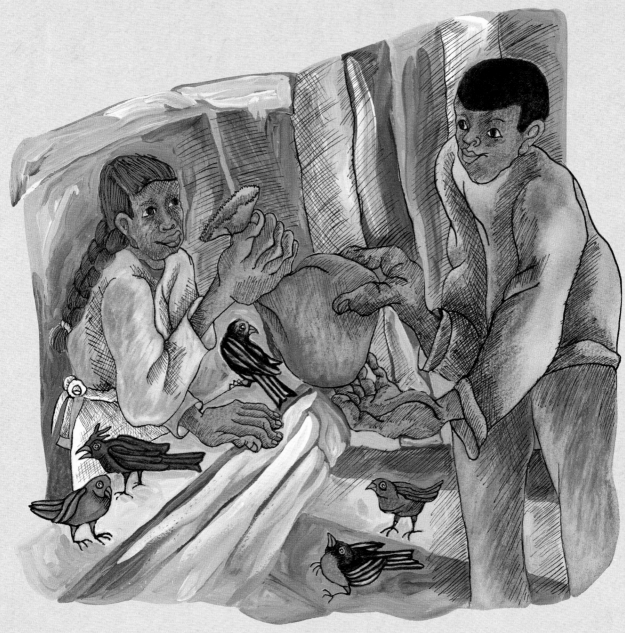

"Keep it," said Raven. "It belongs to you. Because you have been so generous, the bag will never be empty. You will never go hungry."

As he walked toward the gate, Miss Annie looked up to see four ravens swaying on the clothesline.

Suddenly a big gust of wind caught her skirt. It whirled her around and around. Miss Annie Mae and Effie were caught up in a whirlwind. When it stopped, they both went tumbling to the ground.

There was a flutter of wings. Miss Annie Mae's hands shook. The bag shook. Seeds came spilling out.

Five ravens landed in front of her. One held a seed in its mouth and seemed to stare into her soul. Then they all flew away.

Every day Miss Annie Mae takes out her shaking bag. She gives it a good shaking. *"Shake it up! Shake it up! All around!"* Miss Annie Mae sings.

She feeds her birds. Then Miss Annie Mae and Effie Lucille eat. There is always enough.

Sometimes when the wind blows, Miss Annie Mae feels a flutter close by. When she looks into the eyes of the visiting bird, she sees Raven's eyes. Young of age, ancient of spirit.